Sit. Stay. Smile!

We have a winner! Three, actually.
Pippin, Gus, and Scout are the proud, cute
winners of the UnitedHealthcare Children's
Foundation Pic My Pet Photo Contest.
From the hundreds of pet photos entered,
people voted these three as their favorites.
The winners received great prizes, while
kids received medical grants with the
money raised. That's a win-win all around.

Visit uhccf.org to learn about UHCCF
and all its events and contests.

PIPPIN **GUS** **SCOUT**

Sometimes, it takes more than laughter to make us feel great. By purchasing this book, you help UHCCF provide medical grants to families across the United States. These medical grants help children gain access to health-related services not covered, or not fully covered, by their family's commercial health insurance plan. Thank you for making a difference.

Now let's have some fun!

Publication of this book was made possible by the generous support of UnitedHealthcare.

United Healthcare Children's Foundation

ISBN: 978-0-9990394-2-7

Manufactured in the United States of America.
Second Printing.

Publisher: UHCCF/Adventure
Author: Kids across the United States
Contact: UnitedHealthcare Children's Foundation

                 MN017-W400
                 9700 Healthcare Lane
                 Minnetonka, MN 55343

                 1-855-MY-UHCCF (1-855-698-4223)
                 uhccf.org

Find more laughs inside the
"Little Book, Big Laughs"
series at uhccf.org/shop!

Want even more laughs?

Check out all the books in our Little Book, Big Laughs joke book
series. Proceeds from each help fund children's medical grants,
and will keep you laughing for hours.

What is red, white, blue, and yellow?
The Star-Spangled Banana
Miranda S. | Green Bay, WI

Knock Knock. *Who's there?*
Doughnut. *Doughnut who?*
We doughnut have classes during summer.
Gabe B. | Slidell, LA

What is a witch's favorite subject?
Spelling!
Taelon P. | Kannapolis, NC

Find more *Little Book, Big Laughs* books at **uhccf.org/shop**.

. . . .

About UHCCF

UHCCF is a 501(c)(3) charitable organization that provides medical grants to
help children gain access to health-related services not covered, or not fully
covered, by their family's commercial health insurance plan. Families can receive
up to $5,000 annually per child ($10,000 lifetime maximum per child), and do
not need to have insurance through UnitedHealthcare to be eligible.

PRESENTED TO YOU BY:

To: _____

From: _____

My Favorite Jokes Are On Pages:

_____

_____

_____

United Healthcare Children's Foundation

What did the llama see when he looked in the mirror?

His spitting image

Tom F. | Lake Elmo, MN

What do sloths make when it snows?

Slow angels

Rosie W. | Charleston, SC

Did you see they made round bales of hay illegal in Wisconsin?

It's because the cows weren't getting a square meal.

Olive V. | Green Bay, WI

What kind of cat likes his reflection?

A mirror-cat

Josie H. | Rosemount, MN

What do unicorns call their dad?

Pop-corn

Cambria D. | Rosemount, MN

Where do chicken eggs come from?

The grocery store

Payton S. | Kettering, OH

A snake asked his friend, "Are we poisonous?"

His friend said, "Why do you ask?"

The snake said, "Because I just bit my tongue."

Augustus G. | Zimmerman, MN

What did the judge say when the skunk walked in the court room?

"Odor in the court!"

Arianna J. | Tempe, AZ

A cowboy rides into town on Friday. He stays for three days and leaves on Friday. How did he do it?

His horse's name is Friday.

Robert S. | Maple Lake, MN

What do you say to a rabbit on its birthday?

"Hoppy birthday!"

Abby W. | Sugar Land, TX

What day of the week do all fish dislike the most?

Fry-day

Oliver D. | Apple Valley, MN

What do you call a tiny rodent?

Mini mouse

Amber J. | Hacienda Heights, CA

How do you know if there's an elephant under your bed?

Your head hits the ceiling.

Cambria M. | Whittier, CA

What is a shark's favorite sandwich?

Peanut butter and jellyfish

Elliott E. | Chippewa Falls, WI

What Christmas song do animals sing?

Jungle Bells

Cailen J. | Orlando, FL

Why did the bee go to the doctor?

Because he had hives

Leo V. | Minneapolis, MN

What is a moose's favorite ice cream flavor?

Moose tracks

James M. | Wausau, WI

United Healthcare Children's Foundation

What do you call an alligator wearing a vest?

An in-vest-igator

Elijah M. | College Station, TX

What do you call a cow who plays an instrument?

A MOOOsician

Lucy C. | Plymouth, MN

What do you do if your dog chews a dictionary?

Take the words out of his mouth.

Faith F. | Early, IA

Can a wallaby jump higher than a building?

Of course... buildings can't jump.

Becky L. | Minneapolis, MN

What bird plays beautiful music?

A trumpeter swan

Chris G. | Columbia City, IN

Why wouldn't the crab share his sweets?

Because he was a little shellfish

Clark K. | Loomis, CA

Why don't fish like playing basketball?

They are terrified of nets.

Mae R. | Crystal, MN

What do cows say when they get married?

"I MOO!"

Elliott E. | Chippewa Falls, WI

United
Healthcare
Children's Foundation

Do you want to be my Valentine?

You otter!

Colette F. | Bloomington, MN

What did the lamb have for lunch?

A BAAA-loney sandwich

Luke K. | Bloomington, IN

Hippo 1: You look like you're gaining weight.

Hippo 2: That's very hippo-critical of you.

Addie C. | Silver Spring, MD

Why did the monkey cross the road?

Because the chicken retired

Nora M. | Duluth, MN

How do ducks learn to fly?

They just wing it.

Gloria E. | Myrtle Beach, SC

Why do shepherds never learn to count sheep?

If they did, they would always be falling asleep.

Freddy B. | Tampa, FL

What is a grasshopper's favorite sport?

Cricket

Dakota E. | Ida Grove, IA

What do you call a really cold puppy?

A pup-sicle

Jackson W. | Rocklin, CA

United
Healthcare
Children's Foundation

Can a kangaroo jump higher than the Empire State Building?

Of course it can... the Empire State Building can't jump.

Cory K. | Proctor, MN

How did the fish get to the battlefield?

In a tank

Cambria M. | Whittier, CA

What do you get if you cross a pig with a dinosaur?

Jurassic Pork

Georgie G. | South St. Paul, MN

How does a mouse feel after it takes a shower?

Squeaky clean

Angela R. | Sandy Springs, GA

What kind of music do frogs like?

Hip Hop

Adeline F. | Minneapolis, MN

What is a cat's favorite breakfast?

Mice krispies

Gabriella M. | Denver, CO

What is a prickly pear?

Two hedgehogs

Loretta T. | Bloomington, MN

What day is the lion's favorite day to eat?

Chews-day

Miles C. | Charlotte, NC

United Healthcare Children's Foundation

What college do skunks attend?

P.U.

Caitlyn T. | Los Angeles, CA

What kind of cats like to go bowling?

Alley cats

Leo V. | Minneapolis, MN

Fuzzy Wuzzy was a bear,

Fuzzy Wuzzy had no hair,

Fuzzy Wuzzy wasn't very fuzzy, was he?

Oliver B. | Fishers, IN

Where do shellfish go to borrow money?

The prawn broker

Chris K. | Phoenix, AZ

How do you catch a unique rabbit?

Unique up on it.

Cece P. | Inver Grove Heights, MN

What do you call dinosaur policemen?

Tricera-cops

Jackson W. | Arlington Heights, IL

Why was the duck arrested?

It was suspected of fowl play.

Emilio M. | Woodbury, MN

What do you call a pig that can fight?

Pork chop

Oliver B. | Fishers, IN

United Healthcare Children's Foundation

Where do alpacas go on vacation?

Alpaca-poco

Lucy B. | Mankato, MN

Why did the bird fly into the library?

He was looking for bookworms.

Johnny P. | Trenton, NJ

What do sick birds need?

TWEETment

Philipp P. | Chatfield, MN

What do you call a fish with no legs?

A fish

Paisleigh M. | Chippewa Falls, WI

Why are frogs so happy?

They eat whatever bugs them.

Brady J. | Eau Claire, WI

No one is afraid of llama kisses, so why is everyone afraid of the alpaca-lypse?

Savannah B. | Duluth, MN

What did one firefly say to the other firefly?

"I have to glow now."

Macy V. | New York, NY

What do you get when a dinosaur scores a touchdown?

A dino-score

Cabe O. | New Hartford, IA

United
Healthcare
Children's Foundation

What did the tiger say to her cub on his birthday?

"It's ROAR birthday."

Lucy G. | Louisville, KY

Why does a herd of deer have so much money?

Because they have a lot of bucks

Devin V. | Wentzville, MO

Why did the cat cross the road?

He thought he smelled a snack.

Rocky T. | Fullerton, CA

What's a cat's favorite magazine?

A cat-a-logue

Rachel O. | Apple Valley, MN

What kind of a car does a cow drive?

A Cattle-lac

Abigail K. | Raymore, MO

How do you get an octopus to laugh?

You give it ten tickles.

James G. | Bloomington, MN

How did the mule open the door?

With a don-key

Gabe C. | Westfield, IN

What do turtles use to communicate?

A shell-phone

Leo V. | Bloomington, MN

What did the father buffalo say to his son when he left for school?

"Bi-son!"

Dawn S. | Atlanta, GA

Did you hear about the clam that could play the violin?

It had excellent mussel memory.

Chelsea V. | Orlando, FL

Why did the rhino have so much debt?

He couldn't stop charging.

Lou G. | South St. Paul, MN

Why did the mom throw butter out the window?

She wanted to see a butterfly.

Kaylee V. | Menomonie, WI

Where did the killer whale go to fix his teeth?

The orca-dontist

Toby M. | El Reno, OK

What goes tick tock, bow wow, tick tock, bow wow?

A watch dog

Ethan E. | Storm Lake, IA

Why do bee keepers have such beautiful eyes?

Because beauty is in the eye of the bee-holder

Mason E. | Hudson, WI

Why did the leopard refuse to take a bath?

It didn't want to come out spotless.

Adalyn G. | Warrenville, IL

United Healthcare Children's Foundation

Where did the skunk sit in church?

In a pew

Caitlyn T. | Los Angeles, CA

Why did the cow cross the road?

To get to the MOOOsic

Andrew K. | Sun Prairie, WI

What's more amazing than a sheep?

A spelling bee

Jackson B. | Duluth, MN

How do hens dance?

Chick-to-chick

Cindy G. | Monroe, WA

What do you call a gorilla wearing ear-muffs?

Anything you like! He can't hear you!

Franklin V. | Minneapolis, MN

How does the lion greet all the other animals in the jungle?

It says, "Pleased to eat you."

Annie S. | Atlanta, GA

What's the difference between a hippo and a Zippo?

One is really heavy, and the other is a little lighter.

Lyle B. | Round Rock, TX

What did the polar bear eat after the dentist fixed its tooth?

The dentist

Anna L. | Lakeville, MN

What do you call a cow in a tornado?

A milkshake

Tegan D. | New York, NY

How do you catch a squirrel?

Climb a tree and act like a nut.

Clark K. | Loomis, CA

What do bees do if they want to use public transport?

Wait at a BUZZ stop.

Jennifer S. | Boise, ID

What do you call a dinosaur in a car accident?

A Tyrannosauraus wreck

Kristen A. | Bozeman, MT

What state has a lot of cats and dogs?

Pet-sylvania

Aurora S. | Minnetonka, MN

What steps do you take if a tiger is running towards you?

Big ones

Thayden F. | Hull, IA

What is a sheep's favorite game?

BAAA-dminton

Helen E. | Lincoln, NE

United Healthcare Children's Foundation

Why is getting up in the morning, like a pig's tail?

It's twirly (too early).

Sam F. | Lake Elmo, MN

How did the octopus go to the war?

Well-armed

Jake K. | Rapid City, SD

How do you catch a whole school of fish?

With book-worms

Pax C. | Rochester, MN

What is a frog's favorite hot drink?

Hot CROAK-o

Helen E. | Lincoln, NE

Where do otters come from?

Otter space

Cristian J. | Orlando, FL

Where do polar bears store their money?

In a snow bank

Lincoln G. | Duluth, MN

What is a seal's favorite subject in school?

ART, ART, ART!

Reya U. | San Antonio, TX

Who does a frog call if it needs a secret agent?

James Pond

Alex H. | Maple Grove, MN

What is the best way to cook a crocodile?

In a crock-pot

Loftyn A. | Elk Mound, WI

What did one cow to say to the other cow?

"Got milk?"

Rachel O. | Apple Valley, MN

What do you call a lazy baby kangaroo?

A pouch potato

Sophie H. | Saint Marys, GA

What did the tired slug say to the other slug?

"I'm feeling sluggish today."

Andrew K. | Sun Prairie, WI

What did the horse say when it fell?

"I've fallen and I can't giddyup."

Lincoln H. | Bloomington, MN

What do you call a cat who works for Santa?

Santa Claws

Annika P. | Cumberland, WI

What does the head fly do when the other flies aren't working hard enough?

He fires-flies.

James G. | Bloomington, MN

What kind of shoes do frogs wear?

Open toad sandals

Elise W. | Pittsfield, MA

United Healthcare Children's Foundation

What animals are on government documents?

Seals

Colton F. | Barnum, MN

Why don't alpacas like singing with backup music?

They prefer to sing alpaca-pella.

Ellie T. | Waynesville, NC

Which animal makes the best pet?

A cat, because it is PURR-fect.

Camden L. | Cottage Grove, MN

What does a robot frog say?

"Rivet, rivet!"

Madeline S. | St. Louis, MO

Why was the cow sad?

She was MOOO-dy.

Shelby H. | Concord, NC

What do you call a squid with no tentacles?

A sea log

Wrigley P. | Duluth, MN

How can you tell if an elephant is in the refrigerator?

The door won't close.

Angel B. | Jacksonville, FL

I'm sorry I'm not updating my Facebook status. My cat ate my mouse.

Jaes S. | Brainerd, MN

What is a horse's favorite dance move?

The NEIGH NEIGH

Olivia C. | Duluth, MN

I wanted to tell an animal joke, but it's irr-elephant.

Dorine K. | Battle Creek, IA

You have 100 pigs and 100 deer. What are they worth?

A-hundred-sows-and-bucks

Angela S. | Brookfield, IL

Why did the rooster run away?

Because he was chicken

Barrett O. | New Hartford, IA

How did the farmer find his lost cow?

He tractor down.

Mae R. | Crystal, MN

What do frogs drink?

CROAK-a-cola

Ryder O. | Swanton, OH

What did the fish say to the man cleaning his tank?

"Tank you!"

Max G. | Champlin, MN

What happened when the shark got famous?

He became a starfish.

Jacey E. | Hudson, WI

Swan swam over the sea.

Swim, swan, swim!

Swan swam back again.

Well swum, swan!

Douglas W. | Allen, TX

What did one pig say to the other on Valentine's Day?

"Don't go bacon my heart!"

Evelyn H. | Savage, MN

How does a farmer count all of his cows?

With a cow-culator

Brooklyn H. | Phoenix, AZ

Why did the sheep cross the road?

To get a haircut at the BAA BAA shop

Cailen J. | Orlando, FL

Where did the cat go when it lost its tail?

To the re-tail store

Dorine K. | Battle Creek, IA

Why did the firefly get good grades in school?

Because he was so bright

Isaak G. | Minneapolis, MN

What do you call two monkeys who share an Amazon account?

Prime-mates

Mason E. | Hudson, WI

What do you call a camel with no hump?

Hump-free

Reed and Easton J. | San Clemente, CA

United Healthcare Children's Foundation

What kind of haircuts do bees get?

BUZZZZcuts

Mahlia B. | St. Petersburg, FL

How did the panda lose his dinner?

He was bamboozled.

Elisa C. | Lake Katrine, NY

I was going to tell you a cow joke, but it's pasture bed time.

Jesse V. | Nashville, TN

What did the donkey say to the grass?

"Nice gnawing you."

William T. | Waynesville, NC

What do you get when you cross a moose and a deer?

Mickey Moose

James M. | Wausau, WI

Why did Mozart hate chickens?

All they ever say is "Bach-Bach-Bach."

Henrik B. | Kansas City, KS

Two silk worms got in a fight.

It ended in a tie.

Freddy B. | Tampa, FL

What kind of fish eats mice?

A catfish

Miles R. | Crystal, MN

How do you stop a dog who is barking in the backseat of the car?

Put him in the front seat.

William T. | Waynesville, NC

How do bees get to school?

On a school BUZZZZ

Josie H. | Rosemount, MN

You never see elephants hiding in trees. They must be really good at it.

Annika P. | Cumberland, WI

Why did Addie's parents scream when they saw her report card?

Because there was a bee on it

Addie C. | Silver Spring, MD

Why did the cow jump over the moon?

To get to the Milky Way

Vivian R. | Belleville, IL

What do you call a cow that drinks too much coffee?

Over-calf-inated

Micah I. | St. Louis, MO

How do you fit more pigs on a farm?

Build a sty-scraper.

Olivia W. | Reading, MA

Where does a fish keep its money?

In a river bank

Abby E. | Eau Claire, WI

What kind of milk do you get from mini cows?

Condensed milk

Mia P. | Cloquet, MN

Why didn't the teddy bear want any dessert?

Because he was stuffed

Aubrey L. | Winterport, ME

Where do fish hide when it rains?

They don't, they are already wet.

Josie H. | Rosemount, MN

Why was the cow afraid?

She was a cow-herd.

Brayson M. | Herber City, UT

What did the porcupine say to the cactus?

"Is that you, Mommy?"

Marco S. | Little Rock, AR

What was the scariest prehistoric animal?

The Terror-dactyl

Violet H. | Salt Lake City, UT

Have you ever seen a catfish?

No, they have no way to hold the rod and reel.

Henry P. | Green Bay, WI

What do you get from a pampered cow?

Spoiled milk

Gabriella M. | Denver, CO

A guy walks into a costume party with a girl on his back.

The host asks, "What are you supposed to be?"

The guy says, "A turtle, that's Michelle on my back!"

Jojo F. | Lake Elmo, MN

United Healthcare Children's Foundation

How do bears keep their den cool in the summer?

Bear conditioning

Benny P. | Inver Grove Heights, MN

What kind of shoes does a chicken wear?

Ree-BOCK-BOCK-BOCK-BOCK

Kayla J. | St. Louis, MO

What soda do dogs drink?

Pup-si

Bonnie K. | Chicago, IL

What's it called when a cat wins a dog show?

A cat-has-trophy

Rosie W. | Charleston, SC

Why don't seagulls fly over the bay?

Because then they would be bagels

Hailey W. | Palmer, AK

What do you call a lion at the North Pole?

Lost

Pax C. | Rochester, MN

What do you call two birds in love?

TWEET-hearts

Ben S. | Montpelier, VT

What do you get if you cross a centipede with a parrot?

A walkie-talkie

Collin C. | Medford, OR

What kind of vehicle does a lamb drive?

A Lamb-borghini

Ava L. | Phoenix, AZ

Why did the elephant leave the circus?

He was tired of working for peanuts.

Kelly A. | Sioux Falls, SD

Knock knock

Who's there?

Moo

Moo who?

Make up your mind. Are you a cow or an owl?

Adeline F. | Minneapolis, MN

Where do lions sell their unwanted stuff?

At a jungle sale

Henrik B. | Kansas City, KS

Who is a llama's favorite composer?

Wolfgang Llama-deus Mozart

Savannah B. | Duluth, MN

What did one flea say to the other?

"Should we walk or take a dog?"

Henry P. | Green Bay, WI

How do bulls write?

With a bull-pen

Hailey V. | Belle Plaine, MN

United Healthcare Children's Foundation

Which animal do you want to be in winter?

A little otter

Violet H. | Salt Lake City, UT

How does a duck fly?

They just wing it.

Vincent G. | Edina, MN

Which reindeer tries to fly around on Valentine's Day?

Cupid

Gabe P. | Durham, NC

What is big, muddy and sends people into a trance?

A hypno-potamus

Raphael D. | Rosemount, MN

What do you call a line of rabbits that takes a step back?

A receding hare line

Jasper B. | Swanton, OH

What did the teacher say when the horse walked into the class?

"Why the long face?"

Olivia H. | Rogers, MN

What time is it when an elephant sits on your fence?

Time to get a new fence.

Eli C. | Mesa, AZ

Why did the cat run away from the tree?

Because it was afraid of its bark

Madeline S. | St. Louis, MO

Why was the crab arrested?

For pinching stuff

Ken G. | Monroe, WA

What is a frog's favorite year?

Leap Year

William E. | Tulsa, OK

Knock knock

Who's there?

Alpaca

Alpaca who?

Alpaca the suitcase, and you pack the car.

Evelyn I. | Fullerton, CA

What do you get when you cross a turtle with a giraffe?

A turtle-neck

Leo V. | Bloomington, MN

What animal is best at baseball?

A bat

Elizabeth K. | Madison, WI

Knock knock

Who's there?

A cow says

A cow says who?

No, a cow says MOO!

Liam K. | St. Paris, OH

What's green and loud?

A frog horn

Ayub F. | Richfield, MN

Why do owls get invited to parties?

Because they're a hoot

Joy J. | Oklahoma City, OK

What animal has more lives than a cat?

Frogs: they croak every night.

Spencer T. | Roanoke, VA

What do stylish frogs wear?

Jumpsuits

Sophia H. | Minneapolis, MN

What does a hornet do when it's hot?

He takes off his yellow jacket.

Cabe O. | New Hartford, IA

What's a cow's favorite type of music?

MOO-sicals

Miles M. | Eau Claire, WI

What color socks do sloth bears wear?

They don't wear socks, because they have bear feet.

Becky L. | Minneapolis, MN

Where do velociraptors spend their pocket money?

At a dino-store

Mike A. | Hartford, CT

United Healthcare Children's Foundation

What kind of food do you get when you put a duck and mole together?

QUACK-amole

Miles R. | Crystal, MN

Why did the cowboy buy a dachshund?

Because someone told him to "get along little doggie."

Chris G. | Columbia City, IN

What do you call a really old ant?

Ant-tique

Max W. | South Weber, UT

What kind of eggs does a chicken with hiccups lay?

Scrambled eggs

Garrett F. | Eau Claire, WI

What was the pig doing in the kitchen?

Bake-in'

Abriella B. | Chippewa Falls, WI

What did Mario say when he saw an alpaca?

"Don't-a-worry. It's a false-a-llama."

Charlotte B. | Duluth, MN

What does a dog say after it falls down?

"I feel RUFF."

Timothy L. | Lititz, PA

What do you get when you cross a chicken with a cow?

Roost beef

Gloria E. | Myrtle Beach, SC

Why should you not sit by a turkey at Thanksgiving?

Because you will gobble him up

Asher B. | Chippewa Falls, WI

Why did the dinosaur take a bath?

To become ex-stinked

Ken G. | Monroe, WA

Did you know alligators can grow up to 22 feet? But most of the time they just grow 4.

Harrisen G. | Zimmerman, MN

Why should you not write a book on penguins?

Because writing a book on paper is much easier

Alina S. | Cooper City, FL

What animal should wear a wig?

A bald eagle

Chelsea V. | Orlando, FL

What did the queen bee say to the other bees?

"Beehive yourselves!"

Monroe W. | Ida Grove, IA

Did you know that dogs cannot operate MRI machines, but cats-can?

Gabe P. | Durham, NC

What do you do for a blue whale?

Cheer him up!

Sophia H. | Minneapolis, MN

United Healthcare Children's Foundation

My dog ate all the Scrabble tiles and kept leaving little messages around the yard.

Joaquim M. | Atlanta, GA

Why is the number 9 like a peacock?

It's nothing without its tail.

Ben F. | Lake Elmo, MN

Why did the puppy go in the pool?

Because she was a hot dog

Journey M. | College Station, TX

What do you call a great dog detective?

Sherlock Bones

Jack E. | Downers Grove, IL

Why did the dolphin cross the road?

To get to the other tide

Sebastian L. | New Brighton, MN

What did the secret agent cow say to the other?

"Are you udder cover?"

Collin W. | Pittsfield, MA

What do cats like to eat on a hot day?

A mice-cream cone

Dakota E. | Ida Grove, IA

Why did the sheep get in trouble?

He was BAAAd.

Everett G. | Minneapolis, MN

United Healthcare Children's Foundation

Why did the farmer separate the turkeys?

He sensed fowl play.

Midori J. | Cary, IL

I used to look for shellfish at my local beach every day until I pulled a mussel.

Henry E. | Hugo, MN

What is a dog's favorite Christmas song?

Fleas Navidad

Abigail K. | Raymore, MO

What did the octopus say to his girlfriend?

"Can I hold your hand, hand, hand, hand, hand, hand, hand, hand?"

Kiana H. | Gregory, SD

What do you call a pig with three eyes?

A piiig

Georgie G. | South St. Paul, MN

Farmer: What animal has the worst eating habits?

Kid: The pig?

Farmer: Nope. The turkey, because it gobbles everything up!

Angela S. | Brookfield, IL

What was the first animal in space?

The cow that jumped over the moon.

Kolbi J. | El Paso, TX

How does a penguin make pancakes?

With its flippers

Mateo C. | Charlotte, NC

What's black and white and red all over?

A zebra with a sunburn

Lincoln H. | Bloomington, MN

What did the waiter say to the dog when he brought out her food?

"Bone-appetit!"

Natalie L. | Eau Claire, WI

Why did the cat eat the lemons?

He was a sourpuss.

Aurora S. | Minnetonka, MN

I was going to tell you a joke about a big cat, but I would be lion.

Bonnie K. | Chicago, IL

Knock knock

Who's there?

Ladybug

Ladybug who?

Lady, bug someone else for a change, O.K.?

Rosie W. | Charleston, SC

What kind of ant is even bigger than an elephant?

A gi-ant

Winnie V. | Minneapolis, MN

Why do fish live in saltwater?

Pepper makes them sneeze.

Dixon D. | Porter, OK

How do lazy lions pass the time?

By lion around

Miles C. | Charlotte, NC

What do you call a cow that eats your grass?

A lawn MOOO-er

Grace F. | Early, IA

What do you call a wasp?

A wanna-bee

Nathan P. | Cumberland, WI

Why did the dalmation go to the eye doctor?

He kept seeing spots.

Austen H. | Minnetonka, MN

Why do birds fly south for the winter?

Because it's too far to walk

Joaquim M. | Atlanta, GA

Why can't you play cards in the jungle?

Because it's full of cheetahs!

Eloise H. | Edina, MN

How do you catch a unique sheep?

Unique up on it

How do you catch a tame sheep?

The tame way

Aurora L. | Tolleson, AZ

Where do you find a fish in orbit?

Trouter space

Lucy G. | Bloomington, MN

United Healthcare Children's Foundation

What do you call a bear standing in the rain?

A drizzly bear

Vivienne D. | Eau Claire, WI

What kind of crows stick together?

Vel-crows

Chase H. | Lakeville, MN

Knock knock

Who's there?

A parrot

A parrot who?

A parrot who?

Matthew D. | Boca Raton, FL

A lady told her neighbor, "I went to the animal shelter yesterday and got a puppy for my son."

The funny neighbor said, "That was really a good swap."

Bennett D. | Edina, MN

How do chickens leave the building?

They use the eggs-it.

Ken G. | Monroe, WA

What animal carries an umbrella around?

A rain-deer

Elliott F. | Lake Elmo, MN

What bear was President Roosevelt's favorite?

A teddy bear

Marshall M. | Eau Claire, WI

What do you get when a dinosaur walks through a strawberry patch?

Strawberry jam

Cindy G. | Monroe, WA

How did the cow get through the crowd?

She shouted "MOOve!"

Winston C. | Tipp City, OH

What do you call a pile of kittens?

A MEOW-tain

Hadley H. | Brownsburg, IN

What do you call a turtle who loves photography?

A snapping turtle

Leo V. | Bloomington, MN

Why can't the three bears enter their home?

Because Goldie-locks-the-doors

Lexi R. | Oneida, WI

What would happen if pigs could fly?

The price of bacon would go up.

Zac V. | Seattle, WA

What do you call a pair of octopuses that look exactly the same?

I-tenticle

Charlie S. | Green Bay, WI

What do you call a pig thief?

A ham-burglar

Aarav P. | Chandler, AZ

What do you call a dinosaur that won't have a bath?

A stink-o-saurus

Carter C. | King, NC

Why do you bring fish to a party?

Because it goes good with chips

Zac V. | Seattle, WA

What's a pig's favorite ballet?

Swine Lake

Cambria D. | Rosemount, MN

Where do horses go when they're sick?

The horse-pital

Kathleen K. | Atlanta, GA

Did you hear about the racing snail who got rid of his shell?

He thought it would make him faster, but it just made him sluggish.

Gloria E. | Myrtle Beach, SC

What do you get when you mix a sheep and a porcupine?

A nicely knitted sweater

Evelyn H. | Savage, MN

What is the only dinosaur that likes golf?

A Tee-rex

Marco M. | Devine, TX

I called our local zoo to see if they were open, but I couldn't get through because their lion was busy.

Hallie L. | Lawrenceburg, KY

What do you get when you cross a moose with a ghost?

A cari-BOO!

Chase H. | Lakeville, MN

How did the cow blend in with its surroundings?

Cow-MOO-flague

Nicolas B. | San Antonio, TX

Which side of the horse has the most hair?

The outside

Henry P. | Green Bay, WI

What did the cow say when she saw a semi-truck coming?

"MOOve out of the way!"

Lincoln C. | Plymouth, MN

What does a fish say after sharing a new idea?

"Let minnow what you think."

Dawn S. | Atlanta, GA

Why did the chicken cross the road on Thanksgiving?

Because he saw what happened to the turkey

Ellis F. | Fort Pierre, SD

Where do rabbits go after their wedding?

On their bunny-moon

Lyndsay H. | Las Vegas, NV

How do you invite a dinosaur to a cafe?

"Tea, Rex?"

Brody O. | Bloomington, MN

United
Healthcare
Children's Foundation

What kind of turtle flies?

A turtle dove

Natalie L. | Eau Claire, WI

Where do unicorns go to ride the merry-go-round?

A unicorn-ival

Megan L. | Cottage Grove, MN

What is a cat's favorite kitchen tool?

A whisker

Alyssa W. | Jacksonville, FL

Oohh, I know a mouse joke! But, it's probably too cheesy.

Cristian H. | Winston-Salem, NC

Where do owls go to buy their clothes?

The owl-let mall

Tom F. | Lake Elmo, MN

Why do reindeer enjoy doing yoga?

It makes them feel Blit-zen.

Lexi R. | Oneida, WI

What do you call a dog that meditates?

Aware-wolf

Hunter M. | Colton, CA

I know bears can be scary, but some are just un-bear-able!

Ayub F. | Richfield, MN

What did the pony say when he had a sore throat?

"Do you have any water? I'm a little horse."

Devin V. | Wentzville, MO

What weighs two tons and jumps like a frog?

A hoppy-potamus

Loretta T. | Bloomington, MN

What's a dog's favorite food for breakfast?

Pooched eggs

Amelia S. | Yachts, OR

Why do Dasher and Dancer love coffee?

Because they're Santa's Starbucks

Kelly A. | Sioux Falls, SD

Why did the old man not sing at the festival?

His throat was a little horse.

Lincoln C. | Plymouth, MN

Why do cows never have any money?

Because the farmers milk them dry

Dawn S. | Atlanta, GA

Brother: Have you noticed our dog has 8 legs?

Sister: No way, that is impossible.

Brother: It is true. Come, lets count them. Look, the dog has 2 legs in the front, 2 legs in the back, 2 legs in the right side and 2 legs in the left side. A total of 8 legs!

Amber J. | Hacienda Heights, CA

United Healthcare Children's Foundation

What animal can't you trust with your homework?

A cheetah

Raphael D. | Rosemount, MN

Why didn't the chicken cross the road?

Because there was a KFC on the other side

Marco M. | Devine, TX

What do you get if you cross a cow with a Smurf?

Bleu cheese

Jojo F. | Lake Elmo, MN

What do elephants wear to go swimming?

Trunks

Elayne S. | Georgetown, DE

You know what they say about cows?

They're outstanding in their field!

Oliver D. | Apple Valley, MN

What do you get when a chicken lays an egg on a slide?

An egg roll

Myra S. | Salt Lake City, UT

What time is it when a lion walks into a room?

Time to leave.

Dakota E. | Ida Grove, IA

What did the otter say when he and his buddies got in trouble?

"It wasn't me. It was the otter one."

Isaak G. | Minneapolis, MN

What do you call an arctic cow?

An eski-MOOO

Jennifer S. | Boise, ID

What has webbed feet and fangs?

Count Duckula

Maximiliano T. | San Antonio, TX

What do you call a magical owl?

Who-dini

Raphael D. | Rosemount, MN

What happens when two frogs collide?

They get tongue tied.

Salma A. | Weston, FL

Why did the witches' team lose the baseball game?

Their bats flew away.

Loftyn A. | Elk Mound, WI

What do you call a wolf who gets lost?

A where-wolf

Hunter M. | Colton, CA

Why did the hot dog wear a sweater?

Because he was a chili dog

Monroe W. | Ida Grove, IA

How do Spanish-speaking sheep say Merry Christmas?

"Fleece Navidad"

Pamela B. | Crosby, ND

United Healthcare Children's Foundation

What is a pirate's favorite fish?

A swordfish

William E. | Tulsa, OK

What kind of job does a spider have?

He's a web designer.

Cabe O. | New Hartford, IA

Why shouldn't you tell a chicken egg a good joke?

Because it might crack up

Shaelie S. | Brainerd, MN

What did the birdie say at Halloween?

"Twick or TWEET!"

Jacey E. | Hudson, WI

What do you get when you combine a kitty and a fish?

A PURR-anha

Addie C. | Silver Spring, MD

How many skunks does it take to make a stink?

A-pew

Elizabeth K. | Madison, WI

How are a dog and a marine biologist alike?

One wags a tail, and the other tags a whale.

Sofie D. | Franklin, TN

What do you call a horse that likes to stay up late?

A night-mare

Kathleen K. | Atlanta, GA

Why did the cow look at the newspaper?

To find the MOOO-vie listings

Miles M. | Eau Claire, WI

Why did the pig have ink all over its face?

Because it came out of the pen

Mahlia B. | St. Petersburg, FL

What is a sheep's favorite sweet?

Cotton candy

Morgan W. | Cincinnati, OH

Where do tough chickens come from?

Hard-boiled eggs

Richard S. | Concord, NH

Where do mice park their boats?

The hickory dickory dock

Wesley J. | Bloomington, MN

What is a cat's favorite song?

Three Blind Mice

Raymund V. | Chicago, IL

How does a frog feel when he has a broken leg?

Unhoppy

Ariel A. | Richardson, TX

What bird is always out of breath?

A puffin

Kaylee V. | Menomonie, WI

What do you call a sleeping dinosaur?

A dinoSNORE!

Max S. | Aurora, CO

Why should you never rob a bank with a pig?

They always squeal.

Lincoln H. | Bloomington, MN

What do you give a 600-pound gorilla?

Anything it wants

Luke and Grant K. | Bloomington, IN

Why are teddy bears never hungry?

Because they are always stuffed

Meredith D. | Apple Valley, MN

What do you get when you cross a porcupine with a balloon?

Pop

Malia A. | Prior Lake, MN

What kind of bedtime stories do cows read?

Dairy tales

Payton S. | Kettering, OH

Why were the reindeer still in the barn when they were supposed to be with Santa?

They were stalling.

Gabe P. | Durham, NC

Why did the cow cross the street?

To get to the MOOOvies

Anton G. | Duluth, MN

What happened when the turkey fell down?

He got the stuffing knocked out of him.

Chris G. | Columbia City, IN

What do you call a shark with a tie?

So-fish-ticated

Ben S. | Montpelier, VT

What do you get when you cross a snake and a pie?

A pie-thon

Blake M. | Chippewa Falls, WI

What did the shark say to the other shark?

"There's some-fin special about you."

Camden L. | Cottage Grove, MN

What did the Cinderella fish wear to the ball?

Glass flippers

Alma R. | Boulder, CO

What is a lion's favorite state?

Maine

Marco S. | Little Rock, AR

What do sloths like to read?

Snooze-papers

Nathan P. | Cumberland, WI

Which bird steals soap from your bath?

A robber duck

Aubrey B. | Duluth, MN

What do you call a monkey with a wizard's hat and a broomstick?

Hairy Potter

Ariel A. | Richardson, TX

What does an owl dress up as for Halloween?

A knight

Timothy L. | Lititz, PA

What do you call a chicken at the North Pole?

Lost

Leo V. | Minneapolis, MN

What do you call it when one bull spies on another bull?

A steak out

Maverick D. | Eau Claire, WI

What did the duck say to the marshmallow when he was roasting it?

"Stay still so I can put you on my graham QUACKer."

Brooklyn L. | Duluth, MN

Which animal cries the most?

A whale

Charlotte C. | Sugar Land, TX

What did one pig say to the other pig?

"You take me for grunted!"

Joy J. | Oklahoma City, OK

Why does a flamingo lift up one leg?

If it lifted both legs, it would fall over.

Jane W. | Golden Valley, MN

Knock knock

Who's there?

Interrupting cow

Interrupting cow–

Moo!

Zaire F. | Miamisburg, OH

Why would hunting a bald eagle in America be a bad idea?

It's ill-eagle.

Jesse G. | Worthington, MN

Why did the chicken cross the playground?

To get to the other slide

Mike A. | Hartford, CT

Why do cows have hooves and not feet?

Because they lac-toes

Mia P. | Cloquet, MN

What happened when the sloth ate a watch?

It was very time consuming.

Noah H. | Tucson, AZ

Why is a swordfish the best dressed animal in the ocean?

He always dresses sharp.

Henry E. | Hugo, MN

Why are dogs like phones?

Because they have collar IDs

Amelia S. | Yachts, OR

Did you know that cows give more milk if you talk to them?

It goes in one ear and out the udder.

Sarah O. | Kingston, NY

My boyfriend told me to stop acting like a flamingo, so I had to put my foot down.

Lexi R. | Oneida, WI

What do you call a cool octopus?

Tenta-cool

Adalyn G. | Warrenville, IL

What happens when a cow doesn't shave?

It grows a MOOO-stache.

Mia M. | Mondovi, WI

What did the alpaca say to the sad camel?

"Don't worry, you'll get over this hump."

Ellie T. | Waynesville, NC

Why did the snake cross the road?

To get to the other SSSSide

Rylan R. | San Antonio, TX

How much does it cost to fly Santa's sleigh?

Eight bucks, nine during bad weather

Lucy C. | Plymouth, MN

What is the perfect fish?

An angel-fish

Miranda F. | Eau Claire, WI

United
Healthcare
Children's Foundation

Where do whales go to listen to music?

An orca-stra

Wesley J. | Bloomington, MN

What is a dog's favorite instrument?

A trombone

Brady S. | Henderson, NV

What animal sleeps with their shoes on?

Horses

Miranda F. | Eau Claire, WI

What's the most musical part of a fish?

The scales

Cindy G. | Monroe, WA

Why doesn't anyone want to play with the crab?

He is too shellfish.

Everett G. | Minneapolis, MN

What do you call a rabbit with fleas?

Bugs Bunny

Ellie S. | Neenah, WI

Why do the French eat snails?

They don't like fast food.

Kinsley T. | Roanoke, VA

Did you hear the one about the dog who was grumpy?

Well, he must have had a RUFF morning.

Ayub F. | Richfield, MN

United
Healthcare
Children's Foundation

What kind of animal do you bring into battle?

Army-dillo

Addie C. | Silver Spring, MD

Where do cows go on holiday?

MOOO Zealand

Mahlia B. | St. Petersburg, FL

What's another reason polar bears have fur coats?

They would freeze in Hawaiian shirts.

Anna L. | Lakeville, MN

What does a cow sound like that doesn't have any lips?

"OOOO"

Christopher C. | Smithfield, RI

What is the strongest animal?

A snail, because he carries his house on his back.

Franklin V. | Minneapolis, MN

What do you call shaving a crazy sheep?

Shear madness

Kinsley T. | Roanoke, VA

What did the beaver say to the tree?

"Nice gnawing you!"

Malcom B. | Minneapolis, MN

What does a bankrupt frog say?

"Ba-roke, ba-roke, ba-roke."

Landyn S. | Florence, AZ

United
Healthcare
Children's Foundation

How long do chickens work?

Around the cluck

Camden L. | Cottage Grove, MN

What came after the dinosaur?

Its tail

Canyon D. | Herriman, UT

What did the rabbit give his bride?

A 24-carrot diamond

Cambria D. | Rosemount, MN

A crocodile tried to sneak up on his long-legged bird friend to scare him.

The bird said, "Hey, stop being such a stork!"

Luke E. | Vineyard, UT

How does a cat sing scales?

Do-re-MEOW!

Ashlyn T. | Minnetonka, MN

What's the difference between a crocodile and an alligator?

One of them you'll see in a while, and the other one you'll see later.

Lyle B. | Round Rock, TX

How does a hedgehog play leap-frog?

Very carefully

Casey H. | Leeds, NY

What do you call a reindeer on Halloween?

A cariBOO

Finn L. | Lakeville, MN

Which pet is the loudest?

A trum-pet

Isabell B. | Kansas City, KS

What do sheep do on sunny days?

Have a BAA-BAA-cue

Kaylin K. | Flagstaff, AZ

What fish goes up the river 100 miles per hour?

A motor pike

Hailie H. | Rosemount, MN

What did one fish in the ocean say to the other fish in the ocean?

Nothing, they just waved.

Nova D. | Fort Worth, TX

What does a frog eat with his hamburger?

French flies

Emilio M. | Woodbury, MN

Where does Noah keep his bees?

The Ark-hives

Payton S. | Kettering, OH

What did the pig in the desert say?

"Hey guys, I'm bacon out here!"

Isaak G. | Minneapolis, MN

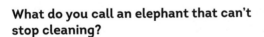

What do you call an elephant that can't stop cleaning?

Cinderella-phant

Isabell B. | Kansas City, KS

Why did the chicken run across the road?

He was late for the Cock-a-doodle-do Express.

Jamaal S. | St. Louis, MO

Why do unicorns love astronomy?

Because they get to study the u-NEIGH-verse

Adeline S. | Artesia, NM

Why don't fish play tennis?

They're scared of the net.

Ava M. | Bayport, MN

Why did the lion spit out the clown?

He tasted funny.

Zaid A. | Weston, FL

What do you call a hard working bee?

A busy bee

D'Anthony M. | Holmen, WI

How do we know that carrots are good for our eyes?

Have you ever seen a rabbit wearing glasses?

Sebastian T. | Palmetto Bay, FL

What sport do cats play?

Hairball

Bryden T. | Eau Claire, WI

What is a frog's favorite game?

CROAK-ay

Myrtle V. | Minneapolis, MN

How do you keep an elephant from charging?

Take away his credit card.

Toby M. | El Reno, OK

What kind of fish only comes out at night?

A starfish

Winnie V. | Bloomington, MN

What do you do if your cat swallows your pencil?

Use a pen.

Kareem A. | Weston, FL

Why did the chicken cross the road?

He was going to the hen-house.

Chayson W. | Tucson, AZ

What do reindeer use to wipe off Santa's sleigh?

Santa-tizer

Finn L. | Lakeville, MN

What is a cat's favorite condiment?

MEOW-onnaise

Luke and Grant K. | Bloomington, IN

Have you heard the joke about the skunk?

Nevermind, it really stinks.

Caitlyn T. | Los Angeles, CA

How much does it cost Santa to park his sleigh and reindeer?

Nothing, it's on the house.

Lucy C. | Plymouth, MN

United
Healthcare
Children's Foundation

What do fish use to take a picture?

A clam-ara

Luke K. | Bloomington, IN

What did the tiger say to the white tiger?

"What's all that white stuff?"

Cailyn W. | Chippewa Falls, WI

What do you call a cat holding a lemon?

A sourpuss

Katie R. | Mesa, AZ

Why did the horse sneeze?

He had hay fever.

Violet H. | Salt Lake City, UT

Why are snakes difficult to fool?

You can't pull their leg.

Becky L. | Minneapolis, MN

What do you get when you put three ducks in a box?

A box of QUACKers

Thayden F. | Hull, IA

Two fish are sitting in a tank.

One looks at the other and says, "Hey, do you know how to drive this thing?"

Winnie V. | Bloomington, MN

Why did the bee get married?

He found his honey.

Noah H. | Tucson, AZ

United
Healthcare
Children's Foundation

What do you get when you cross a bear and a skunk?

Winnie-the-pew

Tom F. | Lake Elmo, MN

Who delivers Christmas presents to baby sharks?

Santa Jaws

Pamela B. | Crosby, ND

Where are fish in orbit?

In trout-er space

Nicholas T. | Miami, FL

What does a cow say to another cow when it wants her to get out of the way?

"MOOOve over!"

Levi L. | Lititz, PA

What did the dog's right eye say to the dog's left eye?

"Between you and me, something smells!"

Myles W. | Green Bay, WI

I have wings. I can fly. I'm not a bird yet I soar through the sky. What am I?

An airplane

Sebastian T. | Palmetto Bay, FL

What do you call a snail on a ship?

A snail-or

Lou G. | South St. Paul, MN

What do you call farm animals that have a sense of humor?

Laughing stock

Bo B. | Orlando, FL

What's a frog's favorite candy?

A lolli-hop

Loretta T. | Bloomington, MN

What sound do porcupines make when they kiss?

"Ouch!"

Eloise H. | Durham, NC

Knock knock

Who's there?

Monkey

Monkey who?

Monkey see. Monkey do.

Ava M. | Bayport, MN

What did one duck say to the other duck?

"You're QUACKing me up."

Brooklyn L. | Duluth, MN

Why are koalas not considered a bear?

Because they have different koala-fications

Cooper S. | Chippewa Falls, WI

What do you call a dog with a fever?

A hot dog

Ava L. | Phoenix, AZ

What time does a duck wake up?

At the QUACK of dawn

Myrtle V. | Minneapolis, MN

United
Healthcare
Children's Foundation

What did the llama get when he graduated from school?

A dip-llama

Lucy B. | Mankato, MN

"Waiter! Waiter! Do you have frog legs?"

"No, I always walk this way."

Noah H. | Tucson, AZ

What do you get when you cross a cocker spaniel, a rooster, and a poodle?

A cocker-poodle-doo!

Nathania B. | Lawrenceville, GA

What do you call a cat who lives in an igloo?

An Eski-MEOW

Brayden A. | De Pere, WI

Why did the chicken play the drums?

Because it had its own drumsticks

Veda A. | Plymouth, MN

When does a fox go "MOO?"

When it is learning a new language.

Nicholas T. | Miami, FL

What is black and white, black and white, and black and white?

A penguin rolling down a hill

Ethan E. | Storm Lake, IA

Why did the dog cross the road twice?

He was trying to fetch a boomerang.

Brielle H. | Phoenix, AZ

What did the snail say when he got a ride on the turtle's shell?

"WEEEEEEEEEEEEEEEEEEEE!!!!"

Olivia S. | Richfield, MN

What did the banana say to the dog?

Bananas can't talk, silly!

Shelby D. | Los Angeles, CA

What does it mean if you find horseshoes?

Some poor horse is walking around in his socks.

Kathleen K. | Atlanta, GA

Why did the cow cross the road?

To get to the udder side

Kinsley T. | Purcellville, VA

Two parrots are sitting on a perch. One bird asks the other one, "Does something smell a little fishy to you?"

Landon L. | Chippewa Falls, WI

What do alpacas say when they meet someone new?

"Fleeced to meet you."

Lucy B. | Mankato, MN

Why is a shark gray?

It ate too many gray-fruits.

Jackson R. | Concord, NC

What do you call a messy hippo?

A hippopota-mess

Emma S. | Jackson, WY

Which animal is white, black, and red all over?

A little penguin

Annie S. | Atlanta, GA

How does a dog stop a video?

He presses the paws button.

Grace F. | Early, IA

What kind of math do owls like?

Owl-gebra

Charlotte C. | Sugar Land, TX

Which country do fish like to go to for a vacation?

Finland

James G. | Bloomington, MN

What kind of story does a mother pig tell her baby?

A pig tale

Amber J. | Hacienda Heights, CA

What is as big as an elephant but weighs nothing?

Its shadow

Kolbi J. | El Paso, TX

What did the alpaca say when he went on vacation?

"Alpaca my bags."

Savannah B. | Duluth, MN

What is a bunny's motto?

Don't be mad, be hoppy!

Lyndsay H. | Las Vegas, NV

United
Healthcare
Children's Foundation

What do you call an animal that lives on land?

A land-imal

Lou G. | South St. Paul, MN

Where do polar bears vote?

The North Poll

Addisyn K. | Schaumburg, IL

Who's the smartest pig in the world?

Ein-swine

Jacey E. | Hudson, WI

What's orange and sounds like a parrot?

A carrot

Dawn S. | Atlanta, GA

Have you heard the story about the peacock?

You haven't? Well, it's a beautiful tail.

Jojo F. | Lake Elmo, MN

What is a cow's favorite color?

BLOOOOOO

Neo M. | Chicago, IL

What did the mommy spider say to baby spider?

"You spend too much time on the web."

Alina S. | Cooper City, FL

Do you know how long dinosaurs lived?

The same as short ones

Richard S. | Concord, NH

What did the chicken egg say to the frying pan?

"You crack me up!"

Hailey V. | Belle Plaine, MN

Why do pandas like old movies?

Because they're in black and white

Thomson L. | Cypress, CA

What is a cat's favorite movie?

The Sound of MEOW-sic

Olive V. | Green Bay, WI

What is a clock's favorite animal?

A dog with a tick

Willa S. | Montgomery, OH

What's a skunk's favorite sandwich?

Peanut butter and smelly

Shelby H. | Concord, NC

What's a dog's favorite pizza?

Pup-aroni

Alex J. | Eau Claire, WI

What do you get when you cross a turtle with a llama?

A turtle neck sweater

Charlotte B. | Duluth, MN

Where does a frog fly his flag?

On a tadpole

Luca G. | St. Charles, MO

What do reindeer use to decorate their Christmas trees?

Horn-aments

Alex H. | Maple Grove, MN

What musical instrument do fish not like?

Cast-a-nets

Caleb B. | West Chester, OH

How do you make a goldfish old?

Take away the "g."

Emma H. | Miami, FL

What is a porcupine's favorite game?

Poker

Leighton S. | De Pere, WI

I told my teddy bear he was cute; he plushed.

Kinsley L. | Cottage Grove, MN

How do apes get around the jungle?

In hot air baboons

Dorine K. | Battle Creek, IA

What do you get when you cross an insect with a bunny?

Bugs Bunny

Adalynn R. | Mondovi, WI

What do you call a donkey with three legs?

A wonkey donkey

Emilio M. | Woodbury, MN

Did Rudolph the reindeer go to school?

No, he was elf taught.

Lucy C. | Plymouth, MN

Why did the bat get kicked out of the cave?

He had a bat attitude.

Adalynn R. | Mondovi, WI

Knock knock

Who's there?

Kanga

Kanga who?

No, kangaroo, silly!

Molly L. | Shipshewana, IN

Where does a witch's frog sit?

On a toadstool

Angela R. | Sandy Springs, GA

What do you call a penguin in the desert?

Lost

Malcom B. | Minneapolis, MN

What do you call a thieving crocodile?

A crook-odile

Grace F. | Early, IA

Why was the lion in trouble?

Because he was lyin'

Carter P. | Ellijay, GA

Why did the dog chase its tail?

He was trying to make both ends meet.

Mason M. | Mondovi, WI

What's a dinosaur's least favorite reindeer?

Comet

Finn L. | Lakeville, MN

Why did the dog stop wagging his tail?

His owner told him to paws.

Aceyon H. | Chicago, IL

How did the cow pay for vacation?

With lots of MOOO-ney

Kelly A. | Sioux Falls, SD

How can you tell which bunnies are getting old?

Look for the gray hares.

Addisyn K. | Schaumburg, IL

What sport is a brontosaurus good at?

Squash

Malcom B. | Minneapolis, MN

Knock knock

Who's there?

Baby owl

Baby owl who?

Baby owl see ya later.

Micah I. | St. Louis, MO

United Healthcare Children's Foundation

There were ten cats in a boat, and one jumped out. How many were left?

None, because they were copycats.

Angel B. | Jacksonville, FL

What is a turkey's favorite dessert?

Peach gobbler

Andrew K. | Sun Prairie, WI

Why don't you see giraffes in elementary school?

Because they're already in high school

Hannah E. | Katy, TX

What actor do alpacas love?

Al-paca-chino

Jackson B. | Duluth, MN

What is a donkey's favorite party game?

Pin the tail on the human

Ben F. | Lake Elmo, MN

How do you get a mouse to smile for a picture?

Say "Cheese!"

Adalynn B. | Chippewa Falls, WI

What did the banana do when the monkey chased it?

The banana split

Kristen A. | Bozeman, MT

What do you call a seagull that flies around San Francisco

A bay-gull

Ronan H. | Jameston, NC

How do you get a squirrel to like you?

Act like a nut.

Colette F. | Bloomington, MN

What does a Norwegian dog say?

"WOOF-da!"

Kinsley T. | Purcellville, VA

What did the bat say to the other bat?

"Hang on!"

Neo M. | Chicago, IL

What's a bee's favorite hat?

A bee-nie

Ronan H. | Jameston, NC

Why did the chicken run away from the table?

Because his mom didn't make macaroni and cheese for dinner.

Ryan B. | Lebanon, OH

Why did the baby chick cross the road?

It was take-your-child to work day.

Elliott F. | Lake Elmo, MN

What do you get when you cross a snow leopard and a tiger?

Burr-GRRR

Bradley A. | Wausau, WI

What is the best way to get in touch with a fish?

Drop it a line.

Joy J. | Oklahoma City, OK

United Healthcare Children's Foundation

What did the mouse say to the other mouse when he tried to steal his cheese?

"That's nacho cheese!"

Sienna B. | Tampa, FL

How do you know how much a fish weighs?

Check its scales.

Nora W. | Farmington, MN

What do camels use to hide themselves?

Camel-flauge.

Emma S. | Jackson, WY

Where do chicken eggs go on vacation?

New Yolk City

Loftyn A. | Elk Mound, WI

Do you know what you call a cow that just had a baby?

De-calf-inated

Alex D. | Phoenix, AZ

What do you call a cow that can't produce milk?

A milk dud

Jackson R. | Concord, NC

Why aren't dogs good dancers?

They have two left feet.

Noah S. | Richfield, MN

What's a snake's favorite day of the week?

SSSS-aturday

Marshall M. | Eau Claire, WI

What kind of animals can open a door?

A mon-key, a tur-key, and a don-key

Alex J. | Midlothian, VA

Why does a panda have two black eyes?

Because it didn't look where it was going

Lilly P. | Green Bay, WI

What country do cats like to live in the most?

PURR-u

Tarin R. | Greensboro, NC

What animal cheats at games?

A cheetah

Ava M. | Bayport, MN

What do polar bears eat for lunch?

Ice berg-ers

Robert S. | Maple Lake, MN

What do you get when you cross a pig with a pineapple?

A porky-pine

Chelsea V. | Orlando, FL

Just finished my first shift as a lion impersonator.

It was a roaring success.

Jacob and Joshua K. | San Antonio, TX

Where did the bull take his date on Friday night?

To the MOOOvies

Kaylin K. | Flagstaff, AZ

United Healthcare Children's Foundation

Where do hamsters go on vacation?

Hamster-dam

Hailey V. | Belle Plaine, MN

What bird can be heard at mealtimes?

A swallow

Jennifer S. | Boise, ID

What do you call a cat wearing shoes?

A puss in boots

Bode Y. | Scarborough, ME

What did the mushroom say to the cow

"I'm a fun-guy."

Rylie M. | San Antonio, TX

Why did the turkey cross the road?

To prove he wasn't chicken

Mae R. | Crystal, MN

What do fish take to stay healthy?

Vitamin sea

Gabriella M. | Denver, CO

Why did the cow dress like a chicken?

So she could cross the road

Myra S. | Salt Lake City, UT

What do you call two spiders who just got married?

Newly-webs

Ben S. | Montpelier, VT

United Healthcare Children's Foundation

What is a rabbit's favorite style of dance?

Hip Hop

Cece P. | Inver Grove Heights, MN

Why don't Lucy Llama and Lacey Llama get along?

Typical llama drama

Ellie T. | Waynesville, NC

What did the duck say to the chef?

"I'm trying to make my QUACKers."

Brooklyn L. | Duluth, MN

How do you say "bye-bye" to a curly-haired dog?

"Poodle-oo."

Brayson M. | Herber City, UT

Why don't bears wear socks?

Because they have bear feet

Riley W. | Palmer, AK

What type of shoes are Kermit the Frog's favorite?

Croaks

Ronan H. | Jameston, NC

What do you get when two giraffes collide?

A giraffic jam

Georgie G. | South St. Paul, MN

Why did the duck cross the road?

Because there was a QUACK in the sidewalk

Arthur L. | Mesa, AZ

What do hedgehogs eat?

Prickled onions

William S. | Cooper City, FL

What game do mice love to play?

Hide and SQUEAK

Pax C. | Rochester, MN

What is a cow's favorite ice cream flavor?

MOOO-nilla

Mason M. | Mondovi, WI

Why do cows wear bells?

Because their horns don't work

Bo B. | Orlando, FL

When do you have to dance like a fox?

When you're doing the foxtrot.

Nicholas T. | Miami, FL

What do you call lending money to a bison?

A buff-a-loan

Angela R. | Sandy Springs, GA

What do you get if you cross a fish with an elephant?

Swimming trunks

Franklin V. | Minneapolis, MN

How does a penguin build its home?

Igloos it together.

Kaylin K. | Flagstaff, AZ

How do you make a baby snake cry?

Take away its rattle.

William S. | Cooper City, FL

Why are tigers terrible storytellers?

Because they only have one tail

Amy L. | Minneapolis, MN

What do ducks watch on TV?

Duck-umentaries

Jesse V. | Nashville, TN

What movies do pandas enjoy watching the most?

They love watching the old movies because the movies are black and white.

Annie S. | Atlanta, GA

What kind of wood barks?

Dogwood

Elayne S. | Georgetown, DE

Why are fish so smart?

They live in schools.

Jayla B. | Houston, TX

What do you get when you cross a bush and a pig?

A hedgehog

Lorraine O. | Chippewa Falls, WI

Did you hear about the guy who got a tattoo of an octopus?

He got inked up.

Jake K. | Rapid City, SD

United Healthcare Children's Foundation

Why did the goat run off the cliff?

It didn't see the ewe turn.

Alina S. | Cooper City, FL

How does a lion steer a canoe?

By using his R-OAR

Miles C. | Charlotte, NC

Why do unicorns listen to polka?

They like to hear uni-cordians.

Megan L. | Cottage Grove, MN

What is a duck's favorite snack?

QUACKers and cheese

Charlie S. | Green Bay, WI

What is a skunk's favorite Christmas carol?

Jingle Smells

Pamela B. | Crosby, ND

What do you get when you cross an octagon with a cat?

An octo-puss

Jax O. | Prior Lake, MN

Why didn't the whale cross over the ruins?

Because it was too fishy

Asher H. | Sanford, FL

What do you put on a sick pig?

OINK-ment

Micah I. | St. Louis, MO

United Healthcare Children's Foundation

Why are hippos so wrinkly?

Because you can't iron them

Lucy C. | Plymouth, MN

What happened when 500 hares got loose on Main Street?

The police had to comb the area.

Emma S. | Jackson, WY

Why are crabs good friends?

Because they are great in a pinch

Alex J. | Eau Claire, WI

What's the difference between a piano and a fish?

You can tune a piano, but you can't tuna fish.

Winnie V. | Bloomington, MN

Why did the sheep get an "F" in math?

Because he is BAAAd at it

Bethany R. | Cibolo, TX

What do you call two barracuda fish?

A pair-a-cuda

Thomas R. | Duluth, MN

Boy: Did you know that elephants do not use computers, but love mobile phones?

Girl: I didn't know that, why?

Boy: They don't like mice.

Amber J. | Hacienda Heights, CA

Why did the turtle cross the street?

To get to the Shell station

Ryan B. | St. Peters, MO

United Healthcare Children's Foundation

What has six eyes but cannot see?

Three blind mice

Raphael A. | Plymouth, MN

How can you tell that it's raining cats and dogs?

When you step in some poodles

Henry N. | Chippewa Falls, WI

What animal gets easily offended?

The chicken: it always gets roasted.

Monroe W. | Ida Grove, IA

Why did the cat go to Minnesota?

He wanted a mini soda.

Kinsley T. | Purcellville, VA

What keys can make you laugh?

Monkeys

Amy L. | Minneapolis, MN

What did the French groundhog see when he woke up?

His château

Jesse V. | Nashville, TN

What do you call it when the alpacas take over the world?

The alpaca-lypse

Xavier S. | Green Bay, WI

What did the flying squirrel say to the flying lizard?

"Do you want to play glide and seek?"

Lyndsay H. | Las Vegas, NV

United
Healthcare
Children's Foundation

Why are elephants wrinkled?

Because they can't fit on an ironing board

Olivia S. | Richfield, MN

What did the turtle say when he crossed the finish line?

"Weeeeeeeeeeeee!"

Max W. | South Weber, UT

What's worse than raining cats and dogs?

Hailing taxis

Johnny P. | Trenton, NJ

What is it about birthdays that make kangaroos unhappy?

They only get to celebrate birthdays in leap years.

Henrik B. | Kansas City, KS

What is a cat's favorite color?

PURRRple

Macy M. | Lakeville, MN

What do Scottish frogs play?

Hop-Scotch

Charlotte C. | Sugar Land, TX

What do you call a quiet sheep?

A shhhhheep

Mason M. | Mondovi, WI

What happens when a frog's truck breaks down?

It gets toad away.

Ella H. | Apple Valley, MN

United
Healthcare
Children's Foundation

What did the crab say to the other crab in the morning?

"Why are you so crabby?"

Reed J. | San Clemente, CA

What goes "OOO OOO OOO"?

A cow with no lips

Will C. | Plymouth, MN

How do whales prepare for a party?

They orca-nise it.

Chris K. | Phoenix, AZ

What do you get when you cross a parrot with a pig?

A bird who hogs the conversation.

Mia M. | Mondovi, WI

Why is a bee's hair always sticky?

Because it uses a honey comb

Spencer T. | Roanoke, VA

Why did the farmer scare the cow?

So he could have a milkshake.

Kaylin K. | Flagstaff, AZ

How do you know if there is a dinosaur in your refrigerator?

The door won't shut.

Canyon D. | Herriman, UT

Where did the sheep go on vacation?

The BAAA-HAAA-mas

Myrtle V. | Minneapolis, MN

What do you get when you cross a sheep dog with a rose?

A collie-flower

Raymund V. | Chicago, IL

What animal should you never play a game with?

A cheetah

Alexis H. | Wrightstown, WI

What did the moose say when he realized he spelled a word wrong on his spelling test?

"I've made a huge moose-take!"

Wesley J. | Bloomington, MN

Why should you never share a bed with a pig?

They hog all the covers.

Brady S. | Henderson, NV

Why are pigs bad drivers?

They are all road hogs.

Evelyn H. | Savage, MN

What do you call a cat with a pot of gold?

A leopard-chaun

Luke E. | Vineyard, UT

What do you call a sad frog?

Unhoppy

Kaylin K. | Flagstaff, AZ

What dogs love taking a long shower?

A shampoo-dle

Rachel O. | Apple Valley, MN

A duck, a skunk and a deer went out for dinner at a restaurant one night. When it came time to pay, the skunk didn't have a scent, and the deer didn't have a buck, so they put the meal on the duck's bill.

Zac V. | Seattle, WA

What can you call an alpaca with a carrot in each ear?

Anything you want, because he can't hear you!

William T. | Waynesville, NC

Why did the zebra go to the art museum?

He needed to repaint his stripes.

Chayson W. | Tucson, AZ

What did the dinosaur put on his steak?

Dino sauce

Benny P. | Inver Grove Heights, MN

Why does a milking stool only have three legs?

Because the cow has the udder

Lyle B. | Round Rock, TX

Why do elephants wear tennies?

Because nine-ies are too small

Sienna M. | St. Paul, MN

How do birds talk to each other?

Through Twitter

Madeline S. | St. Louis, MO

Person 1: My dog has no nose!

Person 2: But how does he smell?

Person 1: Terrible!

Nathan P. | Cumberland, WI

United Healthcare Children's Foundation

What did the turkey say to the computer?

"Google, Google, Google."

Adalynn R. | Mondovi, WI

What do whales eat?

Fish and ships

Kristen A. | Bozeman, MT

Knock knock

Who's there?

Some bunny

Some bunny who?

Some bunny has been eating my carrots!

Jayla B. | Houston, TX

What kind of key can't open doors?

A tur-key

Winnie V. | Minneapolis, MN

What's a cow's favorite day?

MOOO-Year's Day

Isabell B. | Kansas City, KS

Patient: Doctor, doctor! I can't help thinking I'm a goat.

Doctor: How long have you felt like this?

Patient: Since I was a kid!

Collin C. | Medford, OR

Want to hear a cat joke?

I'm just kitten.

Silas J. | Jacksonville, FL

What does a frog say when he has a backache?

"RUB-IT! RUB-IT!"

Marcus J. | Riverton, UT

United
Healthcare
Children's Foundation

What did the grape say when the sloth stood on it?

Nothing, it just let out a little wine.

Annika P. | Cumberland, WI

Where did the bull lose all his money?

At the cow-sino

Oliver D. | Apple Valley, MN

Knock knock

Who's there?

Dolly

Dolly who?

Dolly-fin

Abigail L. | Moncks Corner, SC

Have you heard of the animal that has a human hand?

It's called an arm-adillo.

Jesse G. | Worthington, MN

What kind of vehicle does a mouse drive?

A mini van

Mason E. | Hudson, WI

What do you call an angry monkey?

Furious George

Jaes S. | Brainerd, MN

What do you get when you plant a frog?

A CR-OAK tree

Tegan D. | New York, NY

What do you get when you cross a pig and a centipede?

Bacon and legs

Barrett O. | New Hartford, IA

Why did the dog stay out of the sun?

So he wouldn't be a hotdog

Noah S. | Richfield, MN

What is a dog's favorite city?

New Yorkie

Raymund V. | Chicago, IL

What do you call a sarcastic duck?

A wise QUACKer

Charlie S. | Green Bay, WI

What do ghosts put on their turkey?

Grave-y

William S. | Cooper City, FL

How do you keep a skunk from smelling?

Plug its nose.

Alma R. | Boulder, CO

What do you call a girl with a frog on her head?

Lily

Spencer T. | Roanoke, VA

What do you get if you cross fireworks with a duck?

A fireQUACKer

Amy L. | Minneapolis, MN

United Healthcare Children's Foundation

What do you call a T-Rex that lights off fireworks?

Dino-mite

Zoey R. | Osseo, WI

What did the dog say after the test?

"That was RUFF!"

Austen H. | Minnetonka, MN

What do cats call mice on skateboards?

Meals on wheels

Canyon D. | Herriman, UT

What does a fly do to his brother?

Bug him

Timothy L. | Lititz, PA

What did the dog say when he sat on sandpaper?

"RUFF!"

Miles R. | Crystal, MN

What kind of bird works at a construction site?

A crane

Brady S. | Henderson, NV

Why do ducks have flat feet?

To stamp out forest fires

Why do elephants have flat feet?

To stamp out burning ducks

Sienna M. | St. Paul, MN

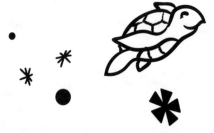

What did the cow say to the chicken eggs?

"MOOOve or get scrambled!"

Lilith K. | Eau Claire, WI

What do you get when you cross a kangaroo with a snake?

A jump rope

Connor B. | Ramseur, NC

Knock knock

Who's there?

Fishy

Fishy who?

I smell something fishy. How about you?

Abigail L. | Moncks Corner, SC

What kind of bees never die?

Zom-bees

Tadeo M. | Berwyn, IL

What do you call a cow that twitches?

Beef jerky

Marco S. | Little Rock, AR

How do rabbits travel?

By hareline

Cece P. | Inver Grove Heights, MN

What is a bird's favorite game?

Beak-a-boo

Faith F. | Early, IA

What did the koala say to the kangaroo?

"Relax...you're a bit jumpy."

Brody J. | El Paso, TX

Why did the cow want to become an astronaut?

So he could go to the MOOn!

Max S. | Aurora, CO

What does an alpaca say when you ask them to go on a picnic?

"Alpaca lunch."

Charlotte B. | Duluth, MN

What do you call a cold dog?

A chili dog

Ava L. | Phoenix, AZ

What do you call a crab with a crown?

A pinch-ess

Brady J. | Eau Claire, WI

What side of the turkey has the most feathers?

The outside

Angela S. | Brookfield, IL

What do you call a fish with two legs?

A two-knee fish

Arthur L. | Mesa, AZ

Why do tigers have stripes?

They don't want to be spotted.

Sebastian L. | New Brighton, MN

United Healthcare Children's Foundation

Why do hummingbirds hum?

They don't know the words.

Aiden M. | Whitman, MA

What's an owl's favorite drink?

Hoot beer

Xavier S. | Green Bay, WI

Why can a chicken coop only have two doors?

If it had four doors, it would be a chicken sedan.

Lucy G. | Bloomington, MN

What's small and cuddly and bright purple?

A koala holding his breath

Macy V. | New York, NY

What did the coach say to the cows?

"Now get out there and give me 2%!"

Lucy G. | Bloomington, MN

What did the dachshund say when he won the race?

"I'm a wiener!"

Ava R. | Holtsville, NY

Why did the otter cross the road?

To get to the otter side

Mateo C. | Charlotte, NC

What do you call a deer with no eyes?

No-I-deer

Faith F. | Early, IA

United
Healthcare
Children's Foundation

Did you hear the one about the evil sheep?

He tried to wool the world.

Kolbi J. | El Paso, TX

What is a polar bear's favorite thing to eat?

Burrrr-GRRRRS

Milan B. | Tampa, FL

What do you call a cold dog sitting on a bunny?

A chili dog on a bun

Chris K. | Phoenix, AZ

How do llamas respond when someone says thank you?

"No prob-llama!"

Jackson B. | Duluth, MN

Why did the horse cross the road?

Because it wasn't stable

Brian R. | Spring Green, WI

What happened to the dog that ate nothing but garlic?

His bark was much worse than his bite.

Thayden F. | Hull, IA

What did the dog say to the flea?

"Stop bugging me!"

Madeline S. | St. Louis, MO

What do you say to a hitch-hiking frog?

"Hop in!"

Lou G. | South St. Paul, MN

What do you call a fish with no eyes?

A fsh

Brycen H. | Wrightstown, WI

Where do werewolves store their things?

In a were-house

Hunter M. | Colton, CA

Why did the bird go to the hospital?

To get TWEET-ment

Johnny P. | Trenton, NJ

What dog keeps the best time?

A watch-dog

Noah S. | Richfield, MN

What did the duck say when he bought the lipstick?

"Put it on my bill."

Brady J. | Eau Claire, WI

What is a horse's favorite sport?

Stable tennis

William E. | Tulsa, OK

Why are cheetahs bad at hide and seek?

Because they are always spotted

Kinsley W. | Palmer, AK

What's white, furry, likes to dance, and wears short leather pants?

A polka bear

Anna L. | Lakeville, MN

Why are giraffes so slow to apologize?

It takes them a long time to swallow their pride.

Alma R. | Boulder, CO

How do spiders communicate?

Through the World Wide Web

Kinsley T. | Roanoke, VA

What do you call a funny chicken?

A comedi-hen

Jane W. | Golden Valley, MN

Why was the dog late for the movie?

He was looking for a barking spot.

Owen G. | Folsom, CA

What do you get when you cross a shark with a snowman?

Frostbite

Elliott E. | Chippewa Falls, WI

What do a shark and a computer have in common?

They both have mega-bites.

Bo B. | Orlando, FL

Knock knock

Who's there?

Raccoon eyes

Raccoon eyes who?

What's the matter? Don't you raccoon-eyes me?

Toby M. | El Reno, OK

United Healthcare Children's Foundation

What do you call a horse that lives next door?

A NEIGH-bor!

Sophia G. | Debary, FL

Why was the bird nervous after lunch?

He had butterflies in his stomach.

Richard S. | Concord, NH

Knock knock

Who's there?

Gorilla

Gorilla who?

Gorilla me a hamburger

Isabel F. | Green Bay, WI

Animal jokes, eh? Toucan play at that game!

Jake K. | Rapid City, SD

Knock knock

Who's there?

Lionel

Lionel who?

Lionel bite you if you don't watch out!

Kambree L. | Altoona, WI

What did one fish say to the other?

"Keep your mouth closed, and you'll never get caught."

Freddy B. | Tampa, FL

How do monkeys get down the stairs?

They slide down the banana-ster.

Shaelie S. | Brainerd, MN

How did the frog burn his tongue?

He ate a firefly.

Lilly P. | Green Bay, WI

Child: Mom, I found a dog at the grocery store today.

Mom: No, what was a dog doing at the store?

Child: Hanging out in the barking lot!

Murphy C. | Middletown, DE

What do you say if you meet a toad?

"Wart's new?"

Winnie V. | Minneapolis, MN

Why did the Easter egg hide?

It was a little chicken.

Mike A. | Hartford, CT

What do you call a dinosaur with a big vocabulary?

A the-saurus

Dawn S. | Atlanta, GA

What did the cat say to the dog?

"Cats rule, dogs drool!"

Ellis F. | Fort Pierre, SD

Why couldn't the pony sing?

She was a little horse.

Hazel B. | Paso Robles, CA

What did the dalmatian say after lunch?

"That hit the spot."

Tadeo M. | Berwyn, IL

Where do cats live?

In a PURRR-ple house on the PURRRR-fect street.

Murphy C. | Middletown, DE

What do you call a sleeping bull?

A bull-dozer

Meredith D. | Apple Valley, MN

What do cows use in text messages?

EMOOOjis

Elizabeth K. | Madison, WI

Knock knock

Who's there?

Cowsgo

Cowsgo who?

No, cows go MOO

Collin C. | Medford, OR

What do you call an elephant in a phone booth?

Stuck

Tegan D. | New York, NY

How many elephants can you put into an empty stadium?

One, after that it isn't empty.

Elayne S. | Georgetown, DE

What did the owl say when somebody knocked on his door?

"WHOOO's there?"

Blake M. | Chippewa Falls, WI

What planet is full of cows?

The MOOOn!

Hallie L. | Lawrenceburg, KY

What kind of horses have six legs?

The ones that are being ridden

Sam F. | Lake Elmo, MN

What do you get when you cross a snail with a porcupine?

A slowpoke

Raphael A. | Plymouth, MN

What do you call a bear with no teeth?

A gummy bear

Thad T. | Louisville, TN

What do you get when you cross a fly, a pet, and a car?

A flying car-pet

Charlotte R. | Indianapolis, IN

What was the unicorn's favorite type of a story?

A fairy tale

Megan L. | Cottage Grove, MN

Jot down your own favorite jokes here!

YOU CAN BECOME ONE OF THE AUTHORS!

_____

_____

_____

_____

_____

_____

_____

_____

_____

_____

_____

_____

_____

_____

_____

_____

_____

_____

_____

_____

_____

_____

_____

_____

_____

_____

_____

_____

_____

_____

_____

_____

_____

_____

_____

_____

_____

_____

_____

_____

_____

_____

_____

_____

_____

_____

_____

_____

_____

_____

_____

_____

_____

_____

_____

_____

_____

_____

_____

_____

_____

_____

_____

_____

_____

_____

_____

_____

_____

_____

_____

_____

_____

_____

_____

FIND OLIVER & HOPE® BOOKS, GIFTS AND MORE AT

Discover fun activities and downloads when you visit Oliver & Hope's Clubhouse at uhccf.org.

uhccf.org/shop

United Healthcare Children's Foundation